O'BRIEN SERIES FOR YOUNG READERS

 panda cubs

 pandas

 panda tales

 flyers

panda series

**PANDA books are for young readers
making their own way
through books.**

Conor's Canvas

GILLIAN PERDUE

• Pictures by Michael Connor •

THE O'BRIEN PRESS
DUBLIN

First published 2007 by The O'Brien Press Ltd,
12 Terenure Road East, Dublin 6, Ireland.
Tel: +353 1 4923333; Fax: +353 1 4922777
E-mail: books@obrien.ie
Website: www.obrien.ie

ISBN: 978-1-84717-043-9

British Library Cataloguing-in-Publication Data
Perdue, Gillian
Conor's canvas. - (Panda series)
1. Painting - Juvenile fiction 2. Children's stories
I. Title
823.9'2[J]

The O'Brien Press receives assistance from

1 2 3 4 5 6 7 8 9 10
07 08 09 10 11 12

Typesetting, layout, editing, design: The O'Brien Press Ltd
Printed and bound in the UK by J.H. Haynes & Co Ltd, Sparkford

Conor loved painting.
It was one of his
favourite things
to do at home.

He would sit down
with the paintbrush in his hand
and close his eyes to **think**.

Can YOU spot the panda
hidden in the story?

When he got
a really good idea,
Conor would dip the paintbrush
into the soft, shiny paint
and get to work!

Sometimes, Conor painted
pictures of people,
like the one of Dad
blowing out the candles
on his birthday cake.

In the painting,
Dad had a huge cake
in front of him.

And his hair nearly touched
the flames of the
thirty-five candles
on the cake.

Sometimes,
Conor painted animals,
like the one of
his pet rabbit, Fungi,
with the long, soft ears.

In school, Ms Keane
let the children do
lots of painting.

But sometimes the others
didn't wash their brushes,
so the paints got
all messy and dirty.
Conor hated that.

One day, Ms Keane
gave the children
some great news.

'We are going to have
our very own art exhibition,'
she said.

'All your Mums and Dads
and Grannies and Grandads
and anybody else you want
can come to the big hall
to see all your paintings!'

'Great!' said Conor.
'I can't wait to do my painting.'

Ms Keane told them
all about famous artists.
Artists used canvas, she said,
so their paintings lasted
forever.

She told the children
to think carefully
about what they would
like to paint.

'You might like to paint
a picture of a person you know,'
said Ms Keane.
'Or your pet?' said Mark.
'Yes,' said Ms Keane.

'Above all, you must
do your best,' she said.

Then Ms Keane
gave the children
a piece of very good news.

'You have no homework
for the rest of the week,'
she said. 'Your work will be
to do your painting!
You must have it in
by Friday.'

All the children
started talking about
their paintings.

But Conor was quiet.
He thought about
his painting all day.

He wanted his picture
to be **big**.
He wanted it to have
lots of colours in it.
He wanted to use
lots of paint.

At home, later that day,
Conor told everyone
about the painting homework.

'We did that when
I was in Ms Keane's class,'
said Laura.
'I painted a picture
of a bowl of fruit.'

'What will you paint, Conor?'
said Dad.
'I don't know yet,'
said Conor.

That night, in bed,
Conor had a lovely dream.

He was walking
inside a painting.

It was full of all the colours
of the rainbow!

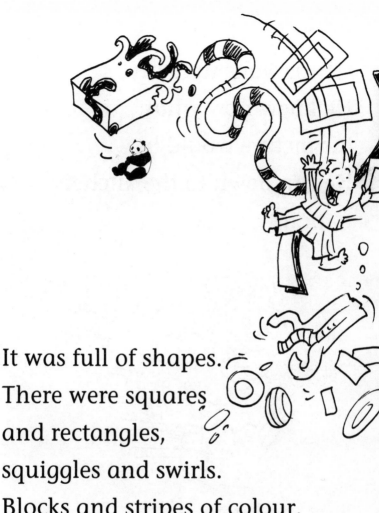

It was full of shapes.
There were squares
and rectangles,
squiggles and swirls.
Blocks and stripes of colour.
Dots and spots.
It was brilliant!

Conor woke up early.
He knew now what
his picture would be.
He ran down to the kitchen
to paint.

First, he knew
he had to use a canvas,
not a piece of paper.

He found a huge white sheet
in the back of a cupboard.

He spread it out
on the kitchen floor.

Next, he took out
every single bottle of paint
that he could find
in the art cupboard.

Then, he took out
the cans of paint
that were in the garage too.

Conor painted
dots and **stripes**.
He painted **swirls** and **curls**.
He painted **squares**
and **triangles**,
circles and **rectangles**.

'This is great!' said Conor.
'**I love painting**.'

Then, he had a great idea.
He began to flick the paint
on to the canvas.
It fell like a tiny shower
of colourful rain.

Then, Conor rolled up his
pyjama-bottoms.
He painted the
soles of his feet.

He painted the left foot purple
and the right one blue.

And he **danced**
all over his painting.

Just then, Mum, Dad
and Laura came
into the kitchen.
They stood staring at Conor
and at his canvas.

'Is **that** your painting, Conor?'
whispered Dad.
His eyebrows shot upwards.

'Is that one of **my good
sheets**?' asked Mum.

'That's not a painting,'
said Laura.
'That's a **mess**!'

Conor smiled at them.
'It's my painting,'
he said happily.
'I'm taking it to school
when it's dry.'

'But –' said Mum.
'But –' said Dad.
'But –' said Laura.

'It's **my** painting
and **I love it**!' said Conor.

Laura glared at Conor.
'You can't take that
to school,' she said.
'They'll all laugh at you.'

Conor cleaned the paint
off his feet.
He didn't say anything.

That morning,
some of the children
brought their paintings
to school.
They had finished already.

The paintings looked great.

Kevin had painted Mark.
He had put in
all Mark's freckles.
'It really looks like Mark!'
said the children.

Sarah had painted
her back garden.
'That's lovely,'
said the children.
'You can see all the
colours of the leaves
on the trees!'

'Remember, all the paintings
must be in tomorrow!'
said Ms Keane.
'I hope everybody
has almost finished!'

Later that day,
Conor looked at his canvas.
It was dry now.
It was really **colourful**.
It was really **bright**.
It was **lively**.

But it needed more.

Conor closed his eyes
and thought.

Then he had a great idea.
He ran into the garage
and got his **bike**.

Then he got a big tray
from the cupboard
and put it on the floor.

He took the lid off
a tin of yellow paint
and he poured the
creamy, shiny paint
into the tray.

Conor rode his bike
on the tray first
and then on his canvas!
He left a bright yellow **print**
of tyre tracks
all over the painting.
The tracks criss-crossed
all over the other colours.

Conor looked at his painting.
'**Brilliant**!' he grinned.

Mum came into the kitchen.
She looked at the painting.
She looked at Conor,
with his bike.
'Did you just cycle
all over your painting?'
she said.

Laura came into the kitchen.
She looked at the painting.
'Now it's even
more of a mess,' she said.
'It looks **terrible**.'

The next morning,
the canvas was dry.
Conor rolled it up and
put it in a bag.
Then he went to school.

Ms Keane and the children
were in the classroom
looking at all the paintings.

There were lots of portraits.

The children had painted
their friends, or their grannies,
or even their pets.

There were beautiful
landscape pictures too.

Josh had painted
sheep in a field.

Jenna had painted
some boats out at sea.

Other children had painted
still-life pictures.
There were fruit bowls and jugs.
There were vases of flowers
and loaves of bread.

'Where's your painting,
Conor?' asked Ms Keane.
'Is it finished?'

Conor smiled at Ms Keane.
He opened up the bag
and took out the sheet.
'Stand back!' he said.
'I need plenty of room
for my canvas.'

Conor took two corners
and walked over to
one side of the room.

He did the same
with the other two corners.
Soon the whole sheet
was spread out on the floor.

'What's it meant to **be**?'
asked Josh.
'Yes, what **is** it, Conor?'
said Kevin.

Conor smiled at them.
He pointed at the canvas.
'It's **my painting**!' he said.

Ms Keane looked at Conor.
'Very unusual,' she said.

All day,
the children were busy
hanging the paintings
in the big hall.

'Now!' said Ms Keane.
'Some very exciting news!
Miss Palette from the art gallery
is coming to visit.
She's going to choose
one painting to hang in
the real art gallery!'

That night, the school hall
was full of people.
They all walked
around the hall,
admiring the paintings.

Mum and Dad and Laura
were there too.
'Oh! There's your painting,
Conor,' said Dad. 'It's great!'

Mum looked at the painting.
'It's so ... big!' she said.

'It's a **mess**, Conor,'
said Laura.
'That one of Sarah's garden
is much better, you know.'

Miss Palette came into the hall.
She was dressed all in black,
but she was wearing
a huge, long, colourful scarf.

'Well,' said Miss Palette.
'These paintings
are wonderful!'

She looked at
the portrait of Mark.
'Excellent!' she said.

She looked at Sarah's garden.
'I love this painting,' she said.

She walked all around
the big hall, looking
at all the paintings.

Then she stood
in front of Conor's canvas.
'What have we here?' she said.

The children gathered around.

'It's not a person,' said Kevin.

'Or a place,' said Josh.

'It's not a picture of anything,'
said Jenna. 'Nobody knows
what it is.'

'It's a bit messy, really,
we think,' said Mark.

Miss Palette said:

'This painting is **colourful**.

And nobody knows what it is.

I love it. Who painted it?'

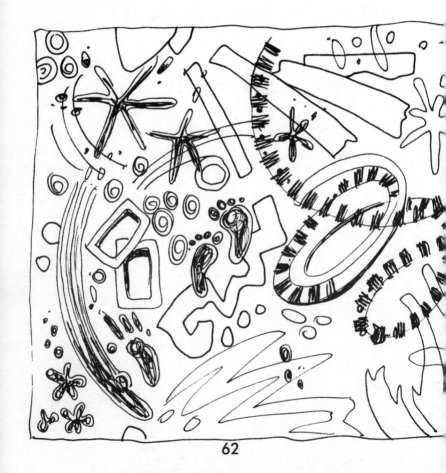

'I did!' said Conor. 'I painted it!'

'It's wonderful, Conor.

It's so **alive**!' said Miss Palette.

'This is the one for the gallery.'

'Hurray for Conor!'
cheered the children.
'Hurray for Conor's canvas!'